The TinyWing Fairies

Suzanne Barton

BLOOMSBURY
CHILDREN'S BOOKS

LONDON OXFORD NEW YORK NEW DELHI SYDNEY

Snow fell softly in Dappletree Woods.
Tiny snowflakes sprinkled the branches, frosting
the leaves and settling like a blanket
at the foot of the Hideaway Tree.

Everything was silent and still . . .

Deep inside the Hideaway Tree it was
cosy and warm. The TinyWing Fairies were
snuggled up in their beds, fast asleep, dreaming
of snowballs and skating and the Winter Fair.

But poor Little Ess — *her* dreams had been
broken by a strange noise . . .

Oooooohooooo Oooooohooooo

Little Ess pulled her blanket up as far as her ears.
"Who's there?" she whispered at the night.

Little Ess didn't like the dark but with
   small, very brave steps, she tiptoed
   across to Marthy's hammock.

"Marthy," she whispered.
   "Wake up. There's a strange
   noise and I'm scared."

"It's just the noise of the woods," said Marthy,
with a yawn. "Nothing to worry about."

But, before she could snuggle Little Ess safely
back in bed, the noise came again . . .

Oooooohooooo Ooooooohooooo

This time it woke up Pip and Tiffin too.
"What was that?" they asked together.

"Hmm, I'm not sure," said Marthy.
"But come on, everyone. Let's go investigating!"

Adventure was Marthy's favourite thing.

As the TinyWing Fairies set out across the sparkling snow, stars twinkled brightly in the sky above.

Oooooohooooo Oooooohooooo

Oooooohooooo

"Everything looks so different,"
gasped Little Ess. "How will we
know which way to go?"

"Easy," said Marthy. "We'll follow the noise.
It seems to be coming from Mrs Mouse's house."

She blinked away snowflakes and peered
into the night. "This way, follow me!"

Mrs Mouse peeped out from behind her door. "Oh, my! What are you doing out on a frosty night like this?" she said. "Come inside and warm your tiny wings."

"We heard a strange noise," Little Ess explained.

"Well, my little ones are squeaky tonight," said Mrs Mouse. "They're so excited about the Winter Fair tomorrow."

Indoors, Mrs Mouse poured everyone some hot berry tea
but, before the fairies could finish, they heard . . .

Oooooohooooo Ooooooohooooo

"*That's* the noise!" said Marthy.
"Thank you for the tea but
we really must go."

"Then wait for me," said
Mrs Mouse. "I'm coming too."

They followed the noise until they reached the tallest tree
in Dappletree Woods and they gazed up into its branches.
"The noise is coming from up there," said Marthy.

The fairies flew up, up, up and, in the treetops,
found Mr Owl with his owlets.

"Have you heard a strange noise?"
asked Little Ess.

"Well, the owlets have been hooting rather a lot," said Mr Owl.
"They're excited about the Winter Fair. I'm sorry they woke you."

"No, that's not the noise," said Tiffin.
"It was more like . . .

OooooohooooO Oooooohooooo

. . . *that!*"

"This way, everyone!" said Marthy.

Before long, they found themselves outside
Mrs Rabbit's cosy burrow.

"TinyWing Fairies out in a snowstorm?" she exclaimed.
"Whatever is the matter?"

"Come in and have some of
Mr Rabbit's carrot cake —
it's freshly baked!"

"We heard a terrible noise,"
said Marthy. "And it's keeping us awake."

"Oh, sorry," said Mrs Rabbit. "It's the bunnies'
first snow, you see, and they're wild about snowballs."

"No, not that noise," said Little Ess . . .

OooooohooooO

"*That* noise!"

"I'm sure it's nothing to be frightened of,"
said Mrs Rabbit, with a friendly smile. "Come on,
I'll help you find out what's going on."

Oooo

Off they all went — scampering, fluttering,
dancing through snowflakes.

OoooooohooOoo OooooOhooooo   OoooooOhooooo OoooooOhooo

"Quick, this way," said Marthy.
She had spotted a clearing . . .

And there, all alone, they found a tiny frost fairy, sobbing loudly.
"So *that's* who's been making the noise!" said Marthy.
"Whatever's the matter?"

"My sleigh is broken," sniffed the Frost Fairy, "and now
I can't deliver the gifts to the Winter Fair."

Oooooohooooo Oooooohooooo

"Oh, what a shame," said Tiffin.
"But don't cry, we'll help you.
Come on, everyone — pull!"

They pushed and they pulled, but it was no use.
The sleigh was stuck fast.

Then Little Ess had an idea — an idea so exciting that she
completely forgot that she was afraid of the dark.
"Wait here," she said. "I'll be back soon."

"You can't go on your own, Little Ess,"
said Marthy. "Wait for me!"

Together Marthy and Little Ess flew
through the night until they came
to Mrs Mouse's house again.

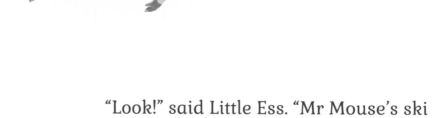

"Look!" said Little Ess. "Mr Mouse's ski
is just right for the sleigh."

Marthy smiled, "Little Ess —
it's perfect!"

Mr Mouse was more than happy to help
so Marthy and Little Ess carried
the ski all the way
back to the others.

Everyone worked by the light of the moon to
mend the sleigh and load it with gifts.

The Frost Fairy was overjoyed.
    "Oh, thank you, thank you all
so much. I'll see you at the
Winter Fair tomorrow."

Back inside the Hideaway Tree,
it was warm and snug, and the night
was quiet at last. The TinyWing Fairies
all slept peacefully in their cosy beds,
including Little Ess . . .

who was dreaming happy dreams
of new friends and the
Winter Fair.

And what a Winter Fair it was! Everyone had fun,
drinking hot chocolate, dancing on the ice
and playing in the snow.

The Frost Fairy gave each of her new friends a wonderful
thank you gift — a shell for Marthy, a silver acorn for Tiffin,
a string of blue petals for Pip and for Little Ess,
a tiny lantern that glowed in the dark.

The TinyWing Fairies hugged their new friend
and said goodbye until next winter.

And, as the snow fell softly in Dappletree Woods,
and the night fell silent, Little Ess led
everyone safely home to bed.

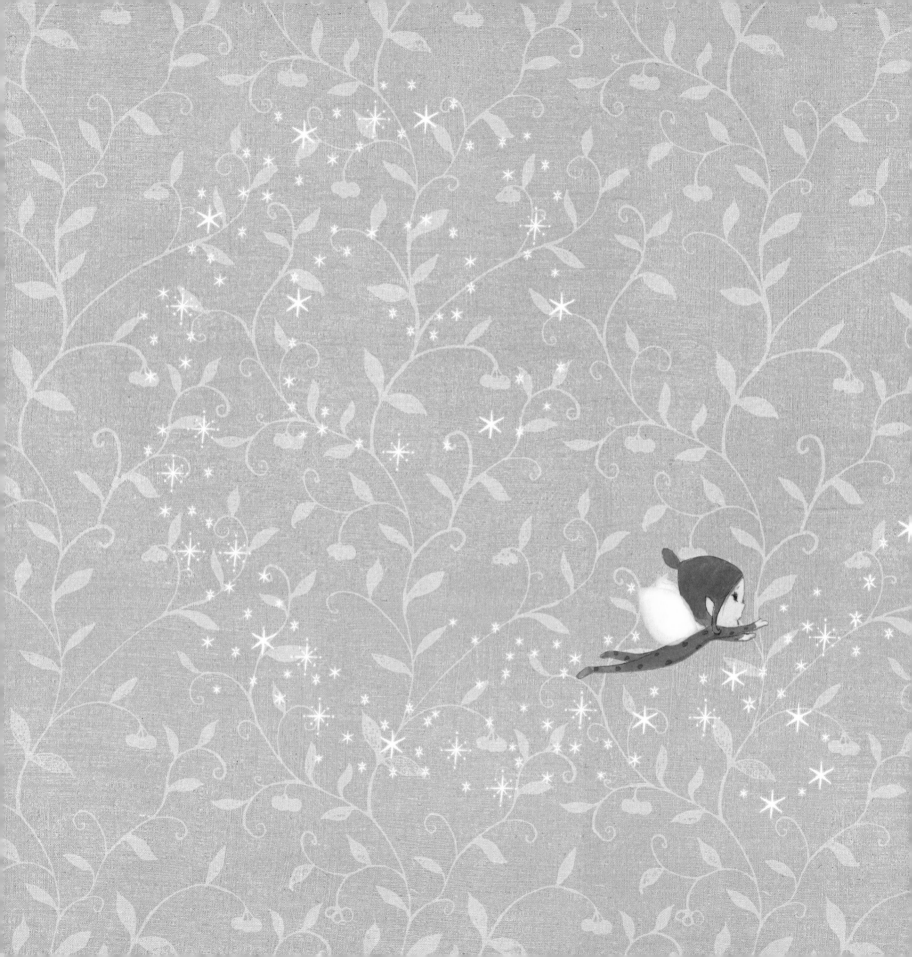